ILLUSTRATED BY chris raschka

# Be BOY BUZZ

bell hooks

JUMP AT THE SUN
HYPERION BOOKS FOR CHILDREN
NEW YORK

To Kenneth Marlowe,
beloved brother,
the boy of my childhood,
remembering moments
of tenderness
and shared joy
**b.h.**

To Renate
**C.R.**

I be boy.

All
bliss
boy.

All fine beat.

All
beau
boy.

Beautiful.

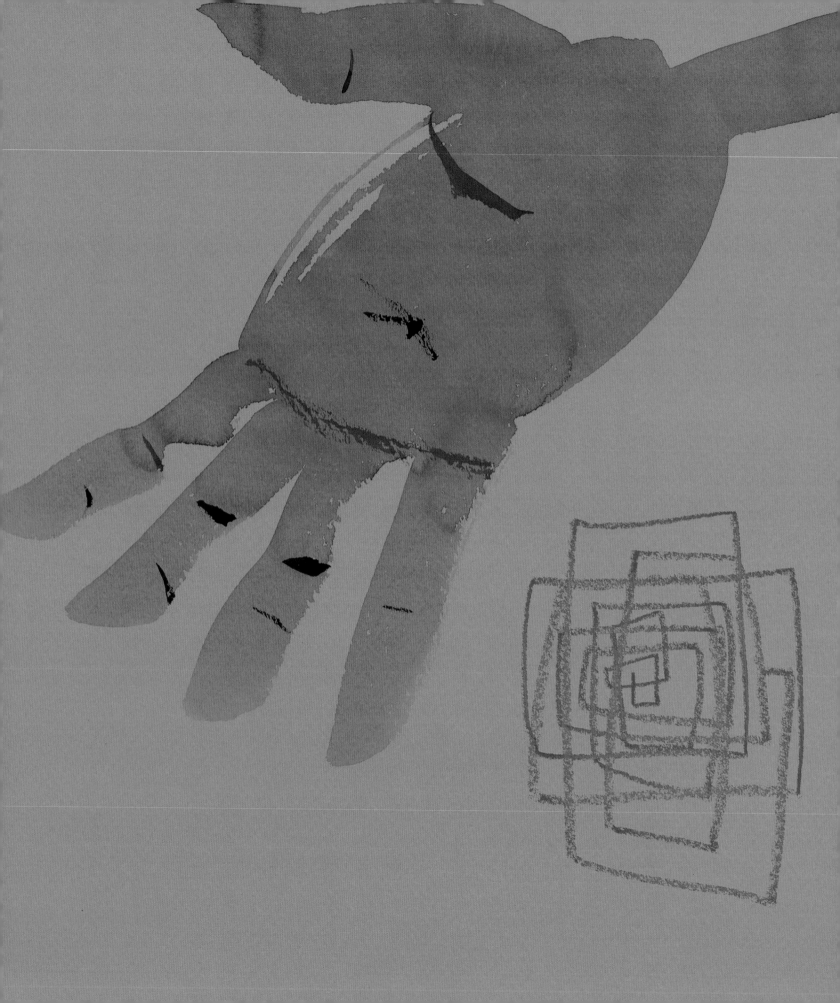

All
bad
boy
beast.

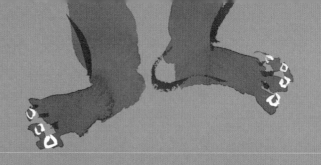

All

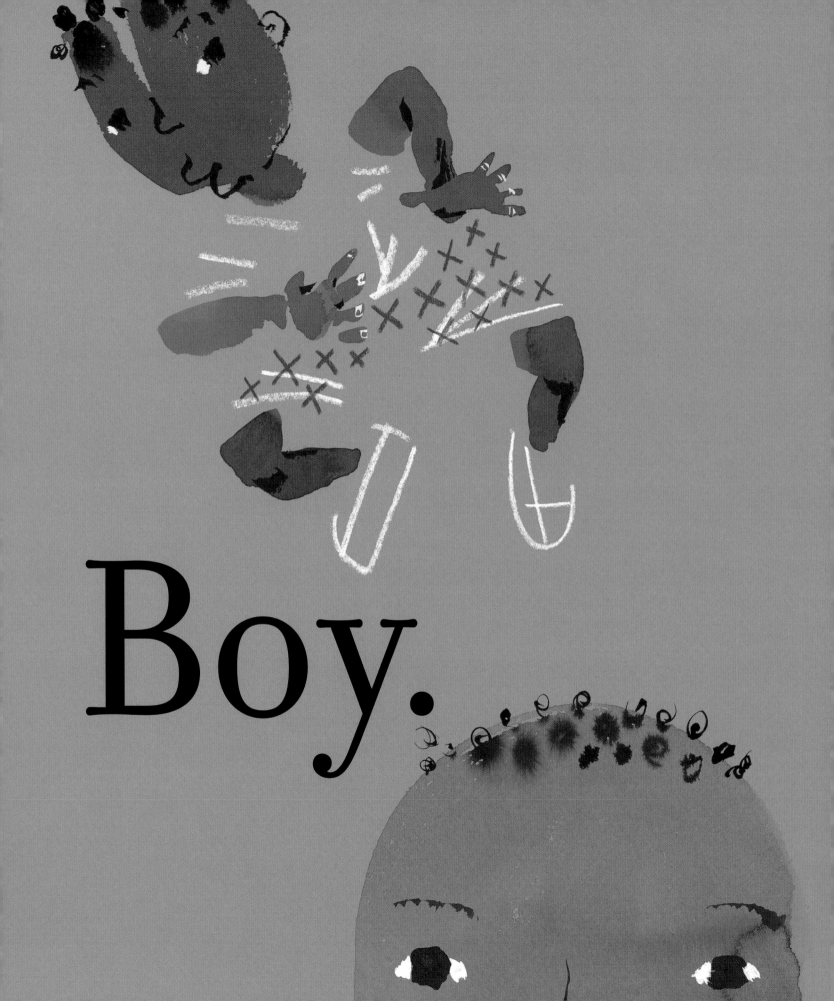

Boy.

I be boy running.

I be boy jumping.

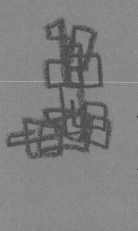

Boy
sitting
down.

I be boy
laughing,
crying,

telling
my story,

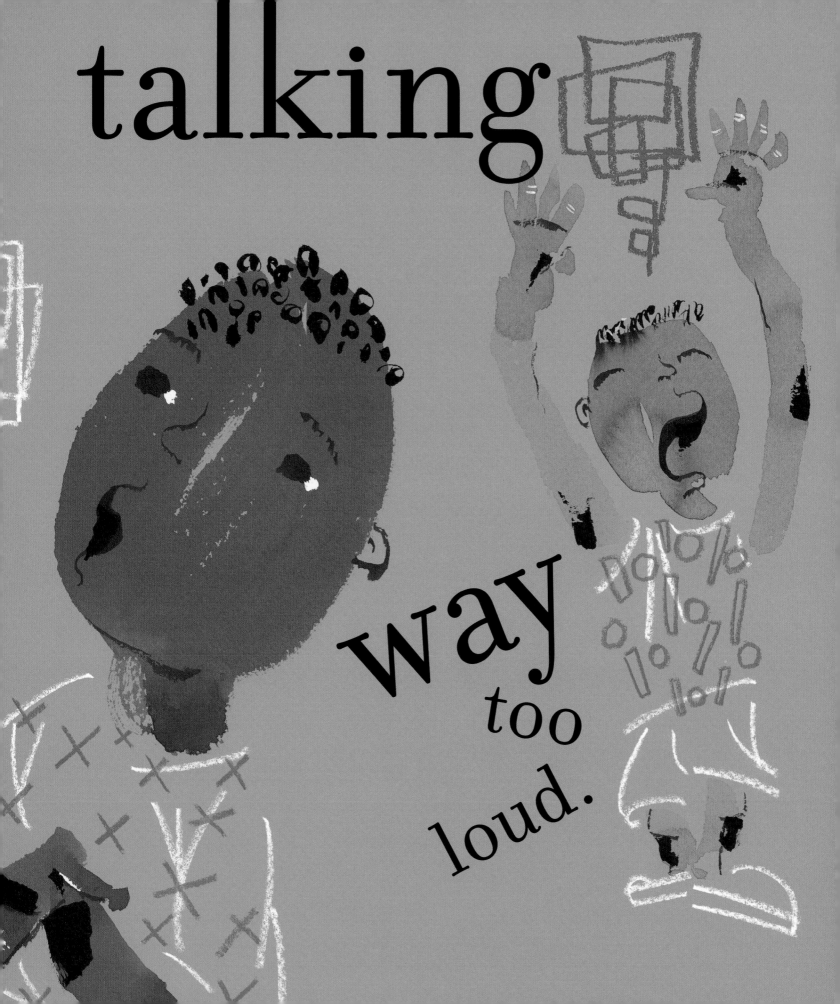

talking

way

too

loud.

Then sitting
      all quiet

still.

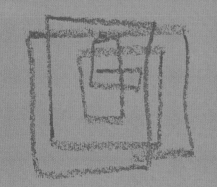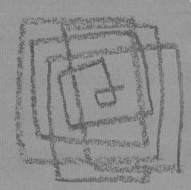

All
boy.

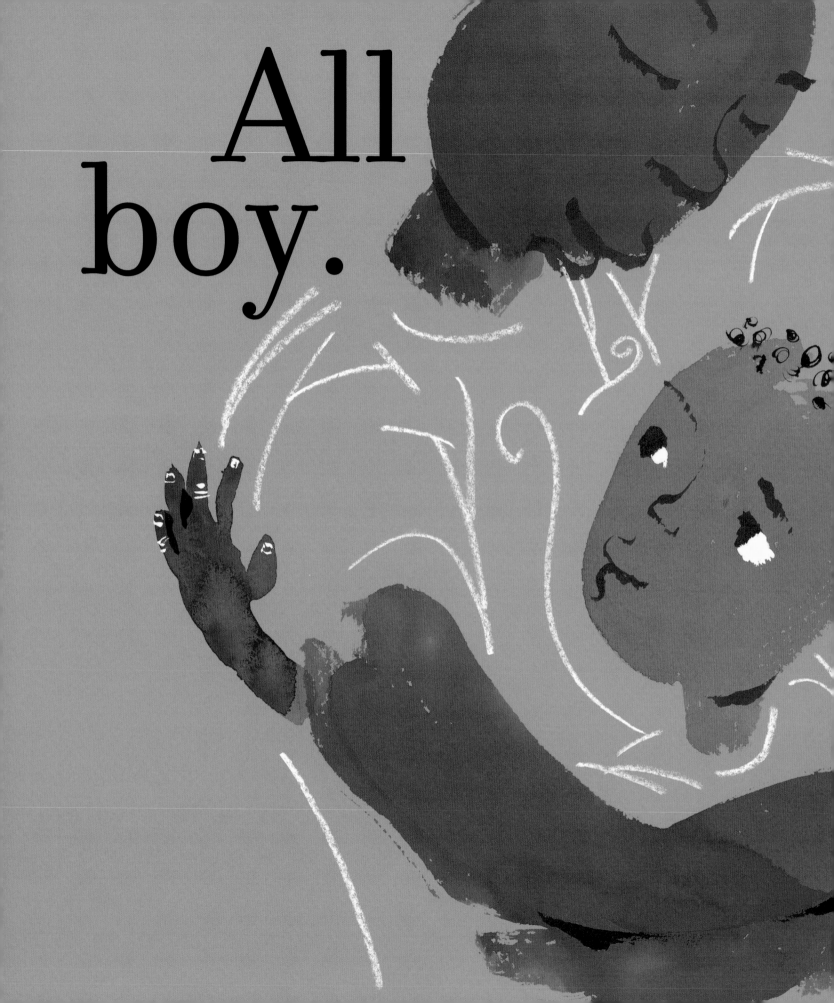

Hug me close.
Don't let me down.

All boy.
Big open
heart.
Sweet
mind.

# All
think
and
dream
time.

Alone
with myself.

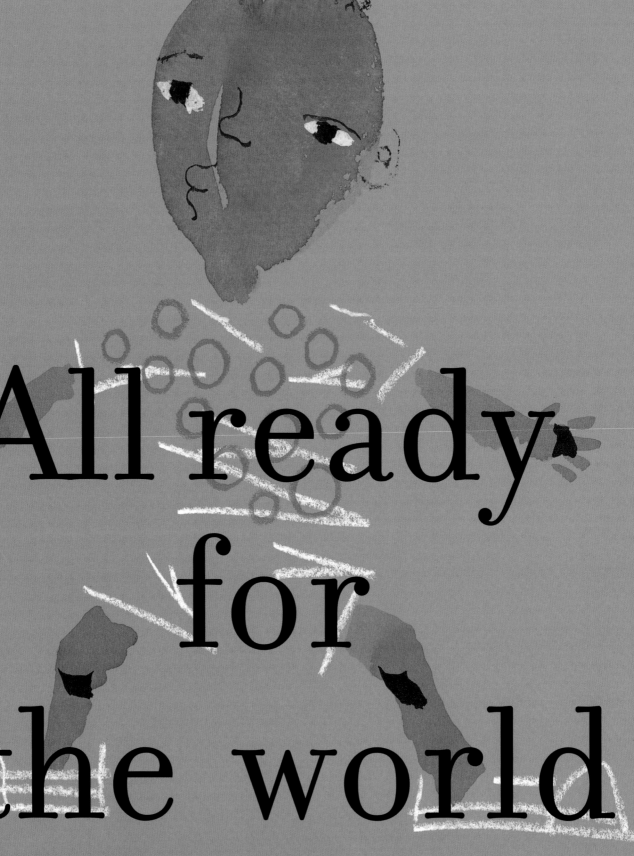

All ready
for
the world

to see

and

play.

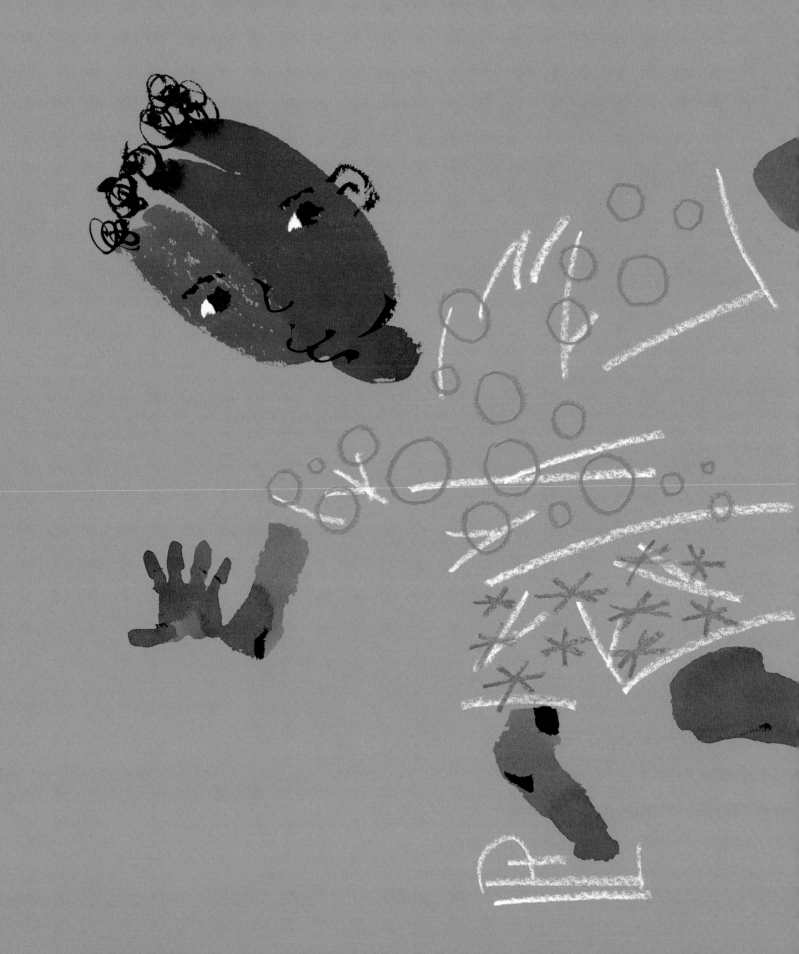

In love
with
being

a
boy.

All
Be
Boy
Buzz.